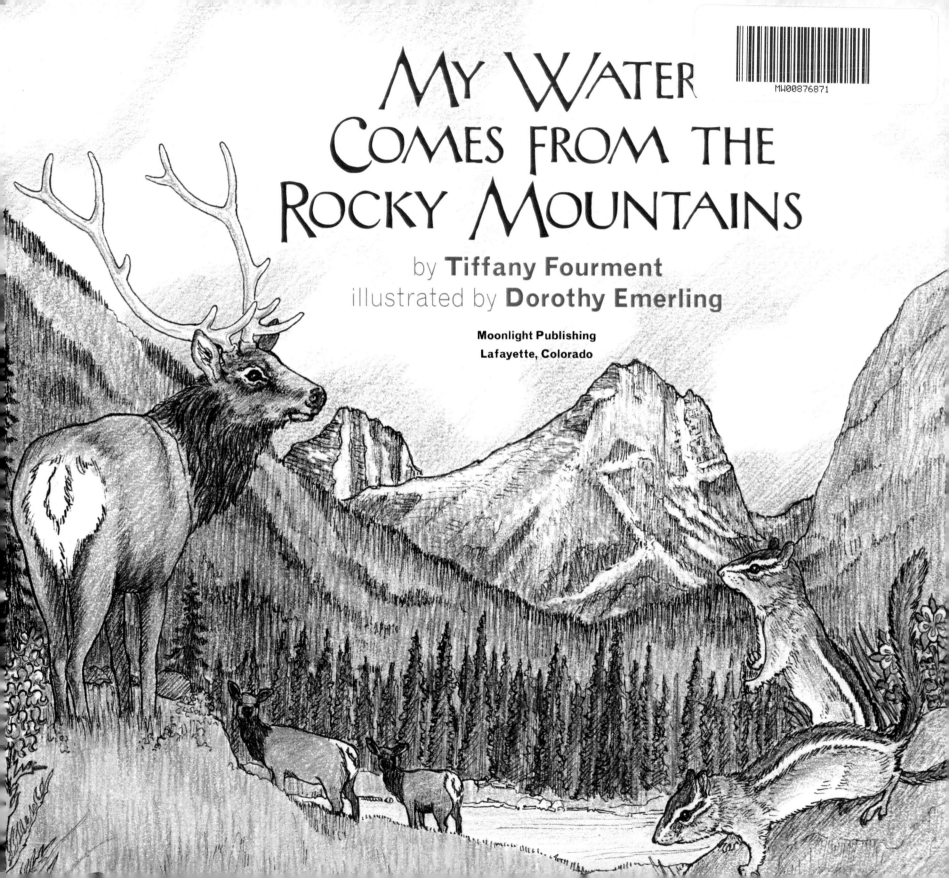

My Water Comes From The Rocky Mountains

by **Tiffany Fourment**

illustrated by **Dorothy Emerling**

Moonlight Publishing
Lafayette, Colorado

This book was prepared through the Niwot Ridge Long Term Ecological Research project of the Institute of Arctic and Alpine Research at the University of Colorado, in recognition of the International Year of Mountain. The author, Tiffany Fourment, participated in an alpine ecology field course taught by Prof. Diane McKnight at the Mountain Research Station.

Support for the book was provided by the K-12 Schoolyard Program of the Long Term Ecological Program of the National Science Foundation.

Moonlight Publishing LLC
2528 Lexington Street
Lafayette, CO 80026
www.moonlight-publishing.com

Distributed by National Book Network

Library of Congress Cataloging-in-Publication Data applied for

ISBN 13: 978-0-9817700-0-0 (cloth)
ISBN 13: 978-0-9817700-1-7 (paper)

Manufactured in Canada.

Acknowledgements

We would like to acknowledge the hard work and dedication of both Mr Kenneth Nova and Ms. Lindsay Weber. Mr. Nova, a fifth grade teacher in the Boulder Valley School District, was instrumental in rewriting and adapting the text and providing a valuable teacher's perspective. Ms. Weber, a graduate of the CU Boulder Environmental Studies masters program, was instrumental in facilitating the development of the children's artwork, working with various organizations to edit and fund the book, and overall guiding the book towards a smooth publication.

The book includes text and illustrations contributed by students in elementary classes in Colorado, Wyoming, Montana, Idaho, and New Mexico. The publisher, author, and illustrator would like to thank the following organizations, schools, and individuals for participating in the preparation of this book.

Organizations

Niwot Ridge Long Term Ecological Research Schoolyard program

National Science Foundation

University of Colorado at Boulder Institute of Arctic and Alpine Research and Environmental Studies Program

Bosque Ecosystem Monitoring Program of the Sevilleta LTER

Denver Water

South Platte River Environmental Education

Boulder Creek Watershed Initiative

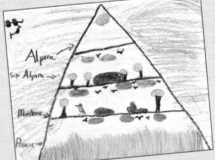

"A pyramid of a watershed."
—Tia-Lanette, Albuquerque, NM

Participating Schools & Teachers

Art Cottage, Boise ID; Teacher: Cathy Mansell

Bixby School, Boulder CO; Teacher: Robert MacKenzie

Bosque School, Albuquerque NM: Teachers Dr Kim Lester and Jonathon Konrad

Dolores Gonzales Elementary, Albuquerque, NM; Teacher: Leslie Lazar

Douglass Elementary, Boulder CO; Teacher: Kenneth Nova

Highland Park Elementary, Sheridan WY ; Teacher: Jackie McMahan

Indian Paintbrush Elementary, Laramie WY; Teacher: Marianne Cook

Meadowlark Elementary, Sheridan WY; Teacher: Christy Spielman

Northside Elementary, Montrose CO; Teacher: Cheryl Isgreen

Poly Drive Elementary, Billings MT; Teacher: Rachel Long

Ponderosa Elementary, Billings MT; Teacher: Rachel Long

Rio Grande Elementary, Belen , NM; Teachers: Delphine Baca, Molly Madden, and Chris Montgomery

Rose Park Elementary, Billings MT; Teacher: Rachel Long

Superior Elementary, Superior CO; Teacher: Mike Wojczuk

Washington Elementary, Billings MT; Teacher: Adriene Loveridge

Individuals

Todd Ackerman
Dr. Clifford Crawford
Dr. Paul Flack
Roxanne Brickell-Reardon
Dr. Diane McKnight
Kenneth Nova
Kimi Scheerer
Lindsay Weber

About the Long Term Ecological Research (LTER) Network

The National Science Foundation's LTER network was begun in 1980 and now includes 26 research sites. The goals of the LTER network are:

• Understanding: To understand a diverse array of ecosystems at multiple spatial and temporal scales.

• Synthesis: To create general knowledge through long-term, interdisciplinary research, synthesis of information, and development of theory.

• Information: To inform the LTER and broader scientific community by creating well designed and well documented databases.

• Legacies: To create a legacy of well-designed and documented long-term observations, experiments, and archives of samples and specimens for future generations.

• Education: To promote training, teaching, and learning about long-term ecological research and theEarth's ecosystems, and to educate a new generation of scientists.

• Outreach: To reach out to the broader scientific community, natural resource managers, policymakers, and the general public by providing decision support, information, recommendations and the knowledge and capability to address complex environmental challenges.

The Schoolyard Series is one component of a broad-scale, long-term effort to combine scientific research and science education through the Schoolyard LTER program. See http://www.lternet.edu/ and http://schoolyard.lternet.edu/ for further information.

The website for this book, http://culter.colorado.edu /MyWater/, presents artwork contributed by all the children in the participating classrooms.

"This is a majestic trout swimming in a stream in the Rocky Mountains going to the Snake River!" —Connor, Boise, ID

One day, way up in the Rocky Mountains, snow fell softly to the ground.

"What's the big deal about that?" you ask. Snow falls all the time in the Rocky Mountains – but do you know what happens to the snow after it's on the ground?

Any guesses? Yes, it melts and turns into water, and that very same snow that falls in those mountains is what comes out of our faucets. When we get a drink of water, take a bath, or turn on the sprinklers in our yard, we are drinking, bathing, and watering our grass with snow.

Sound strange? Well, if you've ever wondered where your water comes from, how it gets to you, or where it goes after we use it, read on, and follow water's journey through a **watershed** as it changes from the fluffy white snow we see in the mountains to the clear liquid we use every day.

"My picture has ducks in the water and elk on the land. The Rocky Mountains are in the background." —Ashley, Billings, MT

Shay, Billings, MT

"Snow becoming water into the river then into a bathtub." —Gigi, Albuquerque, NM

1

Before we start this journey, though, there is one big question: what is a watershed? A **watershed** is an area of land where water collects. The water runs down the mountains and hills, and then drains into creeks or lakes in the valley bottoms. A watershed includes not only the river or lake where the water ends up but also the land that the water flows through. So what does this mean? Well, much like when a dog sheds its hair during the summer, the mountains and hills "shed" water after it snows or rains.

The Continental Divide is a boundary for many watersheds. What watershed do you live in? Well, you are part of the East Slope Watershed if you live east of the Continental Divide, or on what is called the Front Range. Water from this watershed runs east and eventually ends up all the way down in the Gulf of Mexico. That's some journey! However, if you live on the west side of the Continental Divide, you are part of the West Slope Watershed. Instead of flowing east, your water flows west and eventually ends up in the Pacific Ocean.

Just think — the stream running through your neighborhood is not only the water you drink but eventually the water that the rest of the country drinks too. Now that's some big drinking fountain!

"The snow melts and goes down to the river so animals can drink."

—Mason, Billings, MT

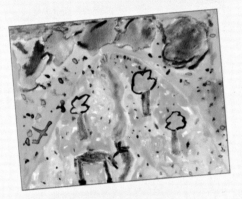

"I drew a mule deer drinking from a river on one side of the Continental Divide. One side goes to the Pacific Ocean and the other goes to the Atlantic Ocean."

—Parker, Sheridan, WY

"My painting is of a shed and snow is falling on the ground."

—Paulo, Boulder, CO

All the water on Earth is part of one big cycle, the **water cycle**.
The journey of water through your watershed is only a small
part of the water cycle.

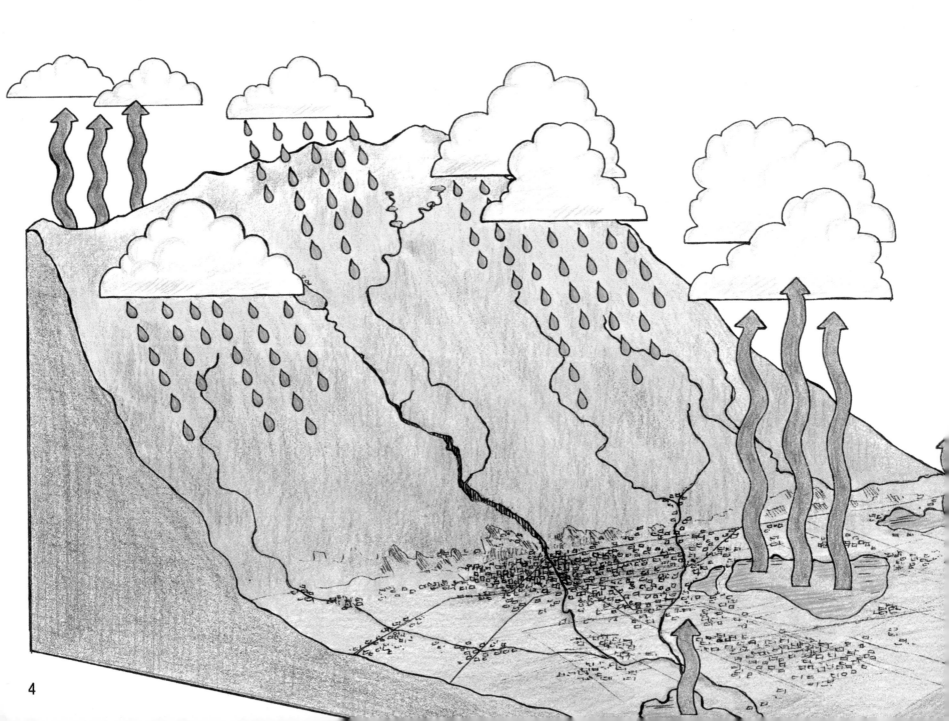

Throughout the whole planet, the sun's heat causes the **evaporation** of water from oceans, lakes, and streams. When water is evaporated, it changes from liquid water that you're used to into a gas called **water vapor**. As the warm water vapor rises into the cooler air higher up, **condensation** occurs and clouds are created. When the clouds get heavy with moisture, the water falls back to Earth as **precipitation**. You know precipitation as rain, sleet, and snow. Precipitation collects again in oceans, lakes, or streams that may be far away from where it evaporated in the beginning. Of course, as we will see, water can go through many different stages in its journey, but whether it's vapor or snow or rain, it is always part of Earth's water cycle.

Now that you know a little bit about water and watersheds, let's take a trip through a Rocky Mountain watershed, from the high mountaintops down to the ocean.

"This is a watershed and this is how water reproduces." —Steven, Albuquerque, NM

"This picture shows the evaporation at the Yellowstone River." —Austin, Billings, MT

The journey of water through our watersheds begins way up in the mountaintops. Here, the snow that falls in the winter collects on the ground and waits for the warm spring sun to melt it.

Snow can also collect on snow fields and **glaciers**, which are large fields of snow and ice located high in the Rocky Mountains. These are areas that don't completely melt in the summer, which is why you and I can see snow-covered mountains even in the middle of summer!

In the winter, scientists measure how much snow has fallen in the Rocky Mountains throughout

Elk

6

the year. The snow they measure is called the snowpack, because as you guessed it, the snow is packed down tight giving the scientists the perfect way to measure how much has accumulated. By checking to see how big the snowpack is, they can predict the amount of water that will come down from the mountains as snow-melt. The larger the snowpack is, the more water there will be in the streams and rivers in the spring and summer and the more water there will be on the long journey down the mountain.

GLACIERS

"Glaciers are collections of snow and ice and because they don't melt or they melt very slowly we can see glaciers through-out the year even in summer."

—Kavita, Boulder, CO

SNOWMELT

"Snowmelt comes from the mountain into the lake in the meadow."

—Brady, Billings, MT

In the spring, the snow starts to melt from the glaciers, mountaintops, and piles of large rocks called **talus**, which are at the very, very top of the Rocky Mountains. As the snow melts, it trickles downward through an area called the **alpine tundra,** which has many small plants with pretty flowers that bloom in the summer. This is an area that is on the highest part of the mountains and is so cold and windy that only special plants or animals can survive there, ones that do not live anywhere else.

Ptarmigan

"My picture shows wind and rain."
—Anthony, Billings, MT

"The snow falling onto the Rocky Mountains."
—Morgan, Albuquerque, NM

There aren't any tall trees that live in the alpine tundra because the high winds and cold temperatures are too much for them. The tall pine trees that you see every day would just freeze and blow over in this tough climate. The plants that do grow in the alpine tundra are rooted tight into the mountain and grow in small clumps very close to the ground where they are more protected from the wind.

Only a few special animals live in the alpine tundra year-round. They include the yellow-bellied marmot, pika, and white-tailed ptarmigan (pronounced tar-mi-gan). They must have special **adaptations** to help them survive in this cold, windy place. The water that drips and trickles through the rock fields on the alpine tundra is a friendly companion of the pika, a small creature that looks like a chubby squirrel without a long tail. CHEEP CHEEP – as the pika scurries among the rocks, its high-pitched call sounds almost like a bird chirping.

Pika

Yellow-bellied marmot

THE ALPINE TUNDRA

"The alpine is a nice place with big hills and beautiful mountains and lots of animals and green grass." —Weston, Boulder, CO

PIKAS

"Pikas are commonly called rock rabbits, coneys and whistling hares. —Mitchell, Montrose, CO

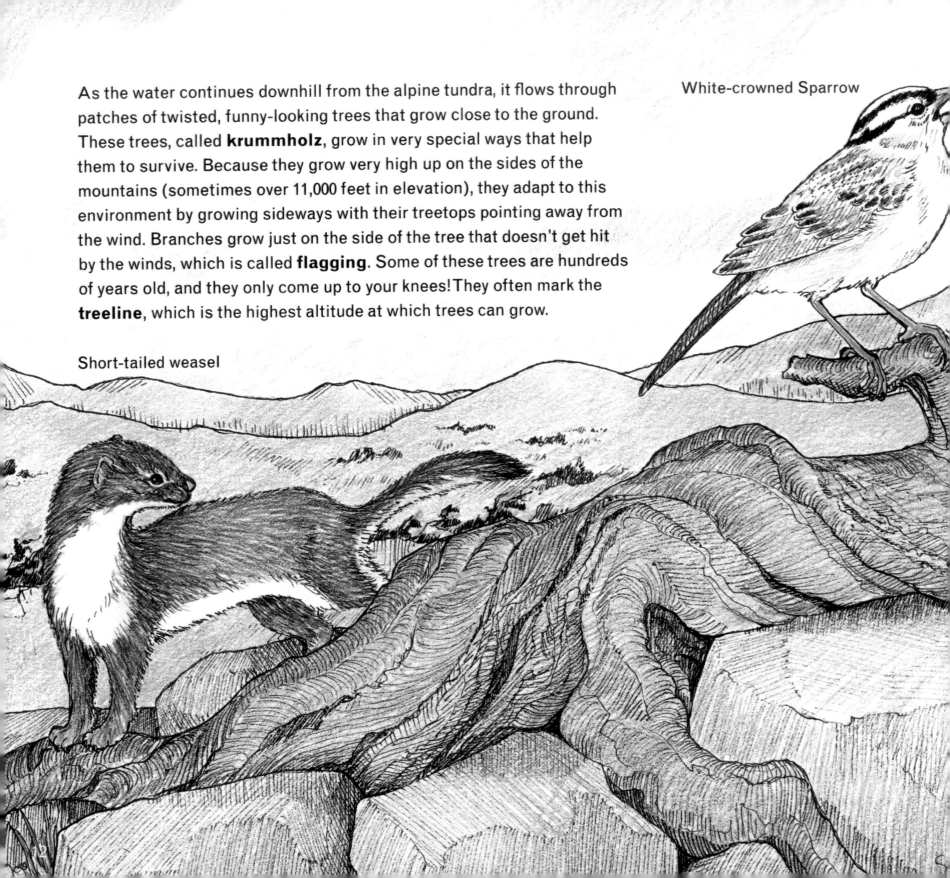

As the water continues downhill from the alpine tundra, it flows through patches of twisted, funny-looking trees that grow close to the ground. These trees, called **krummholz**, grow in very special ways that help them to survive. Because they grow very high up on the sides of the mountains (sometimes over 11,000 feet in elevation), they adapt to this environment by growing sideways with their treetops pointing away from the wind. Branches grow just on the side of the tree that doesn't get hit by the winds, which is called **flagging**. Some of these trees are hundreds of years old, and they only come up to your knees! They often mark the **treeline**, which is the highest altitude at which trees can grow.

White-crowned Sparrow

Short-tailed weasel

Snowshoe hare

FLAGGING

"Because of the strong wind, the branches grow only on one side."   —Erinn, Sheridan, WY

KRUMMHOLZ

Krummholz is a twisted tree that lives in high elevation. It is short so it doesn't have to fight the wind.   —Grant, Boulder, CO

13

As the water keeps flowing downward, it enters the subalpine forest of larger, more "normal-looking" trees. Since they don't live in harsh windy conditions like the krummholz trees, they grow taller and straighter. In this forest, the water that has been trickling along the ground starts to collect in small streams and ponds where animals can take a drink. The subalpine **life zone** provides habitat for the pine martin, snowshoe hare, the mountain lion, and birds of all shapes and sizes.

Mountain lion

Great horned owl

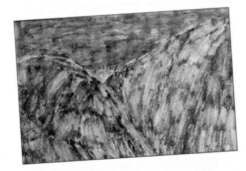

"My picture is of a little creek in the mountains. In the sky there is a sunset." —Natalie, Boise, ID

"My picture is a mountain lion beneath an overhang with rocks." —Anessa, Boulder, CO

"Pine Martins live in the mountains. They look like ferrets but they are orange like foxes. They live in trees most of the time and catch squirrels."
—Lane, Sheridan, WY

From these small streams and ponds, the water starts to flow into larger ones as it moves down the mountains.

Red-tailed hawk

Some streams flow into **reservoirs**, which are large, human-made lakes with a dam at one end that traps and stores the water until it is needed Some of the water from the reservoirs flows into even larger streams and some goes through pipes to a water treatment facility.

At the water treatment facilities, the water is treated to make it safe for people to drink. Water that is not piped to treatment plants is released into streams that continue to flow through the watersheds.

Reservoirs and Dams

"This painting is of a dam and a river in a rainstorm."
—Daniel, Billings, MT

"I like boats because I like to go on them and hear the sound of the beautiful water." —Miguel, Superior, CO

17

Mule deer

Water can flow through several types of landforms as it
heads down the mountains. Sometimes the water pours and
splashes over waterfalls with a crashing ROAR. Creeks also
flow through mountain meadows and rush through steep
canyons.

Below the subalpine life zone, we enter the **montane** life zone. Many plants and animals such as foxes, coyotes, and chipmunks live in this area. They depend on the creeks and streams for food, water, and shelter too. Oh look! A deer that has been grazing nearby has gone down to the water for a drink.

ANIMALS IN THE MONTANE ZONE

"In my picture I drew a red fox. It lurks around in the Rocky Mountains."
—Cloie, Sheridan, WY

"A deer in the woods by the clear mountain water."
—Josephine, Laramie, WY

Red fox

Gray squirrel

Mallard ducks

People use creeks in these areas for fishing, rafting, and kayaking. —Tara, Billings, MT

SPLASH !

"This relates to a watershed because this man is kayaking down a waterfall."

—Amanda, Sheridan, WY

As the creeks of the East Slope leave the mountains, they flow through many towns and cities along the Front Range. If you live here, you will often notice that the creeks are lined with cottonwood trees that grow along the banks of the river. These are the trees that release their seeds in little fluffy tufts of "cotton" that we see floating through the air in the spring. Other trees such as aspen, pine, and fir trees also grow in this area.

Over on the west side of the Rocky Mountains, the creeks of the West Slope begin to flow through areas full of juniper and pine trees. These plants are able to survive in the cold, dry climate here.

21

Now remember the water that was piped into the treatment facility from the streams and reservoirs? Well, that water has been treated to make it clean for us to drink and now comes out of our faucets and hoses. Think about all the times you use water during the day!

WHERE DOES IT GO?

Water that we use in our toilets, sinks, and showers ends up in sanitary sewers and is piped to a different kind of treatment facility where it is cleaned and released back into the creeks and rivers. Another type of sewer is called a storm sewer, or storm drain. Some water, like the water that runs down the sides of the street after a big rain, runs directly into the creeks through these storm drains without being cleaned by a treatment facility. Because this water hasn't been cleaned, it's important not to dump oil and other pollutants into storm drains, because that's the same water that our animals and plants drink.

Brown bat

"These storm drains wash city water down to the lakes, rivers, and oceans."

—William, Boulder, CO

As the water continues on its trip down through the Front Range creeks, streams, and rivers, the land starts to change again. The pine and fir trees disappear, and the creeks flow onto the plains through the **prairie** life zone. There are not many trees in the prairie. Instead, grasses thrive in the plains, since they can survive the drier weather there.

Because of this, prairies are often called grasslands. Some prairie grasses can grow up to 8 feet high!

Coyote

The wildlife living in this habitat changes too. Animals such as prairie dogs, ferrets, burrowing owls, hawks, and antelope live on the prairie, and yes, you guessed it, they depend on the creek for water, too! Yippp yipp yipp, YEOWWWW...a coyote's call is answered by another.

On the journey down the West Slope, the water begins to wind through canyons that can be so deep that it is hard to see the water below. Some water becomes part of huge reservoirs like Lake Powell. These reservoirs can be so big that people live on them in houseboats!

Prairie dogs

"Prairie dogs need water to live and what they eat also needs water to live."
—Dylan, Sheridan, WY

"My picture is a picture about burrowing owls. One is standing next to a hole. The other is in a hole peeking out."
—Allison, Boulder, CO

WEST SLOPE CANYONS

"The Black Canyon of the Gunnison is found in Montrose, Colorado. Its Painted Wall is the largest rock wall in Colorado."
—Mandy, Montrose, CO

"The eagle's nest is in a canyon that has been eroded by water for centuries."
—Tahira, Sheridan, WY

Farmers on both sides of the Rocky Mountains provide us with food and may depend on reservoirs and creeks to irrigate their crops. To **irrigate** means to supply land or crops with extra water. The corn that you buy at a local farmers' market might have been grown with water from the very same creek that flows through your town or city!

Western meadowlark

Some farmers use fertilizers to help their crops grow faster and pesticides to keep bugs from eating their crops. These chemicals can dissolve into the irrigation water, and this water then goes back into the creeks and rivers. So it is important that the chemicals be used carefully. In towns and cities, there are also pollutants that can get into the Rocky Mountain creeks. These pollutants can come from runoff from roads or chemicals applied to lawns, and as you guessed it, end up getting into our own water supply.

"My project is about irrigation."
—Jacob, Sheridan, WY

Did you know that some water collects under the ground? No surprise, it's called **groundwater**. Groundwater collects under the soil in the spaces between rocks, sand, and gravel. An **aquifer** is the underground layer of rock and gravel that contains the groundwater. Aquifers can be small, or they can cover hundreds of square miles like the Ogallala Aquifer. This aquifer is so big it lies beneath parts of Wyoming, Colorado, Nebraska, Kansas, Oklahoma, New Mexico, Texas, and South Dakota. Wow! Now that's a lot of water!

Many people rely on groundwater. For example, farmers may rely on groundwater that they pump out of the ground

Great blue heron

Frog

to irrigate their crops, and many cities and rural households dig wells to use groundwater for drinking and other uses, such as washing and bathing. What do you use water for?

As East Slope creeks flow toward the prairie, they meet up with larger streams and become part of the larger watershed. These creeks and streams flow into even larger rivers, such as the South and North Platte, the Arkansas and the Missouri. Most of this water eventually reaches the Mississippi River, one of the longest rivers of the world. From there it runs all the way to the Gulf of Mexico and then to the Atlantic Ocean.

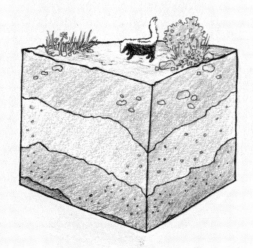

Raccoon

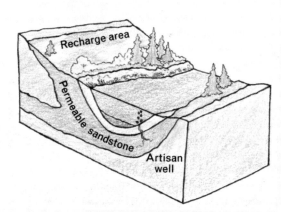

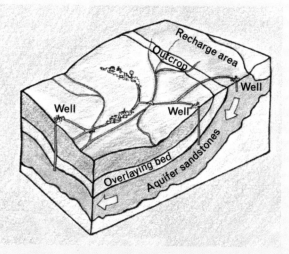

"It has rivers leading to other rivers. All the rivers are leading into the main river." —Skylar, Billings, MT

"My picture is about the Yellowstone River flowing after it has rained."
—Cameron, Billings, MT

What happens to the water that flows down the other side of the Continental Divide? Creeks that flow down the West Slope of the Rocky Mountains join up with larger rivers such as the Colorado, the Snake, and the Columbia, and then head toward the Pacific Ocean. It's a big journey no matter which side of the mountains you live on, but one that the whole country benefits from, and you're right in the middle of it all!

When the water gets to one of the oceans, what happens then? That's right! As the sun rises in the sky to warm the new day, the water cycle starts all over again. Some of the water evaporates out of the ocean, condenses into big fluffy clouds, and eventually, when it gets cold enough, falls as snow. And way up in the Rocky Mountains and in your backyard, snow falls softly to the ground, and the journey begins again.